116

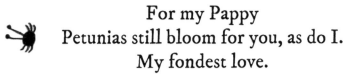

For my Pappy
Petunias still bloom for you, as do I.
My fondest love.

Thanks Stephen, and Theo.

E.H

The Little Gardener © Flying Eye Books 2015.

This is a second edition.

First published in 2015 by Flying Eye Books, an imprint of
Nobrow Ltd. 62 Great Eastern Street, London, EC2A 3QR.

Published in the US by Nobrow (US) Inc.

ISBN: 978-1-909263-43-7

Order from www.flyingeyebooks.com

It didn't look like much,

but it meant everything to its gardener.

It was his home. It was his supper.

It was his joy.

Only, he wasn't much good at gardening.

It wasn't that he didn't work hard.

He worked hard,

very, very hard.

He was just too little.

But there was one thing that did blossom in his garden.

It was a flower.

It was alive and wonderful.

It gave the gardener hope and
it made him work even harder.

He worked all morning.
He worked all afternoon.

He worked all night.

Still, the garden was dying.

He would have no home.
He would have no supper.

He would have no joy.

One night, feeling tired and sad, he made a wish.

No one heard his little voice,

but someone saw his flower.

It was alive and wonderful.

It gave the someone hope.
It made the someone want to work harder.

The next day the gardener was weary and slept the whole day.

He slept the whole week. He slept the whole month.

And when he finally awoke,

it had been just long enough for something to change.

This is the garden now.

And this is its gardener.

He doesn't look like much,
but he means everything to his garden.